Bella the Buck-toothed Ballerina

Written by
Amanda Montoni

Illustrated by
Cydney Bittner

Red Penguin
BOOKS

Bella the Buck-toothed Ballerina
Copyright © 2022 Amanda Montoni
All rights reserved.

Illustrations by Cydney Bittner

Published by Red Penguin Books
Bellerose Village, New York
Library of Congress Control Number: 2022920133
ISBN
Print: 978-1-63777-306-2
Digital: 978-1-63777-307-9

*Dedicated to all of the dreamers inside of us
And to my parents, for always encouraging me
to follow my dreams.*

"Okay, little ballerinas, time to start class!"
Miss Annie calls from the classroom door.

Bella immediately runs to the barre

and starts practicing her positions.

"Come on, girls! To the barre!
Time for our pliés!"
Miss Annie calls again.

Maddie, a girl in class, stands next to Bella
and says, "Practicing?
You're gonna need it."

Miss Annie starts leading the warmups. "Okay, everyone. First position! Toes out!"

"Hey, Bell-o! You'll never be a Ballerina with teeth like that! Ballerinas don't have big spacey teeth like yours!"

This hurt Bella's feelings. How could someone be so mean?
Miss Annie notices Maddie talking and says

"Maddie, we're in third position now."
Maddie quickly adjusts her feet to have the
right foot slightly in front of her left.

After the class finishes their pliés and tendus, Miss Annie instructs everyone to line up for 'Across-The-Floor.'
Maddie purposely ends up right by Bella in line.

"Hey, Buck-y, I bet you're not good enough to beat me to the wall!"

Now Maddie is giving Bella's teeth nicknames!

This made Bella feel upset.
Maddie is right.
Ballerinas don't have buck teeth.

"Time for bourrées!"
Miss Annie shouts happily.

Maddie takes off like a rocket.
Bella is clearly going to lose this bet.

"Maddie! Slow down! This is not a race!
And turn out your toes, like Bella!"
Miss Annie shouts.

This makes Maddie stop in her tracks.

When Miss Annie says it is time to
work on arabesque, Bella gets so excited.
It is her favorite step!

Miss Annie places Bella front and center of the classroom. She puts Maddie in a spot right next to her.

"Plié, arabesque." And all of the little ballerina arms gradually grow into a beautiful diagonal line, but Bella's arms are floating.

Miss Annie says "Everyone! Look at Bella!
She is floating! Just beautiful!
Bella, can you do an arabesque by yourself
for the class?"
This makes Bella feel special.

Maddie sees how beautiful Bella is doing, and decides to say one more mean thing to Bella when Miss Annie goes over to the stereo to play some music.

"You're too ugly to be a ballerina!"
Maddie shouts loudly as she walks up to Bella.

Instead of getting upset, Bella decides that she won't let Maddie's mean words upset her anymore.

She turns around, looks Maddie in the eyes and says "Maybe I am ugly on the outside, but I'm not ugly on the inside. Just you wait.
I'm going to become a ballerina!"

As Miss Annie turns around to address the class,
she addresses Maddie instead.
"Maddie, you know the rule. Less talking in class."

"But! Bella was too!" Maddie pleads.

"I don't want to hear any 'buts'!
Maybe you should follow
Bella's example. Back to your spot.

Okay, class!
Arabesques to music!
... and 5, 6, 7, 8 ..."

As soon as the music starts to play,
Bella forgets about Maddie

And floats through her arabesques with a big shiny

buck-toothed smile glistening across her face.

She is beautiful inside and out.

Acknowledgements

First and foremost, my parents. Without their support and encouragement, I don't know where I would be today. Thank you for putting me into my first dance class. You gave me a love that will last a lifetime. Thank you to Ms. Jan and Ms. Jeanne. You have and continue to teach me so much about the art and appreciation of dance. Without you two, my life-time love would not have blossomed into what it is today. All of your kindness, support, and teachings will stick with me for the rest of my life. Without you, this book wouldn't be possible. To the Kickstarter backers, I can't thank you enough. Thank you for believing in Bella's story. Lastly, I would like to thank Red Penguin Books and Cydney Bittner for all of their beautiful work to make this dream of mine a reality.

Keywords Section:

Barre: This is a structure dancers use to work on balance, technique, posture, and stretches. It is often used in the beginning of classes for warmups that include plié and tendu.

Plié: This means "to bend." Ballet dancers bend their knees to make their legs look like a diamond shape. Pliés are used constantly in ballet.

First Position: The basic and first out of five different ways ballet dancers arrange their feet. In this position, the dancer zips their legs together, the heels of their feet touch, but their toes are pushed apart to make their feet shaped like the letter "V."

Second Position: This is the second out of five different ways ballet dancers arrange their feet. In this position, the dancer's toes are still pushed out to make a "V" shape, but their heels are now apart.

Third Position: This is the third out of five different ways ballet dancers arrange their feet. In this position, the dancer's toes are still pushed out to make a "V" shape, but one foot is placed slightly in front of the other. The heel of the foot in front touches the arch of the foot behind.

Keywords continued:

Tendu: Whenever a ballet dancer moves their foot, they must tendu or "point" their toes. The dancer slides their foot until their heel lifts off the ground. The ball of their foot and toes are curled under, leaving only the big toe touching the ground. The foot should be weightless, and easy to lift. These can be done in any direction from any position.

Across-The-Floor: This is a warmup and exercise in dance classes. Dancers do steps from one side of the room to the other to practice technique while traveling, or dancing across the floor.

Bourrée: These are known as little tiny steps on the balls of a dancer's feet. It is a way to travel while dancing. They can be done in any position.

Arabesque: This is a step in which a dancer slides to put weight on one foot, tendu the other (on the floor or in the air), and extend their arms to make a diagonal line.

About the Author

After being known as "Miss Amanda" for the last 10 years or so, Amanda Montoni has ventured into the writing world. She has published 3 poetry collections, and has been featured in numerous anthologies. She has written plays, short stories, monologues, poems, and essays, but since then, she decided to take her dance teacher skills and put them to creative work in the form of children's literature.

"Bella the Buck-Toothed Ballerina" is the culmination of experiences Amanda has seen as a student, a teacher, and a Director/Choreographer. She wears many many hats, but this new one holds a very special place in her heart.

www.amandamontoni.com

CPSIA information can be obtained
at www.ICGtesting.com
Printed in the USA
LVHW072054220723
753181LV00011B/32